"Happy holidays!" Mickey and his friends shouted. They were in Donald's airplane just before Christmas on their way to see the snow-covered mountains.

Everyone but Donald sang and told silly jokes. Donald was too busy flying the plane. After all, flying was serious business.

"Gosh," said Mickey, "I think we'd better head back before it gets dark."

"No problem," said Donald.

Just then, the engines began to sputter, and the plane dropped lower in the sky. Donald stared at the controls.

"Uh—Donald? I think you've just run out of gas," said Mickey.

The gang held their breath as
Donald prepared to land. Suddenly,
the plane caught a gust of air and
glided down, landing with a giant

THUD!

"Wh-wh-where are we?" asked
Minnie with a shiver.

The friends peered out the frost-
covered windows. Snow stretched
endlessly in all directions.

"We're lost," moaned Daisy.

"But not for long," said Goofy,
reaching into his pocket.

"I've got my trusty compass right
here. Gawrsh, we'll be somewhere
in no time!"

Everyone huddled together to try to stay warm. But the fierce winter wind began to blow. Soon, ice and snow swirled around the desperate little group.

"I don't want to worry anyone," said Mickey, rubbing his hands together, "but I think we're caught in a blizzard!"

"Maybe we can go for help," suggested Minnie.

"Wait," said Daisy, "I think I hear something."

Everyone stood quietly and listened. A strange crunching sound got louder and louder.

"Wh-wh-who's there?" whispered Donald hiding behind Mickey.

"It's me, Jitters," said an elf who appeared from behind a huge mound of snow. "Who are you?" the curious elf continued.

After a relieved Mickey made the introductions, Jitters invited them all to come home with him.

"Come in out of the cold," Jitters called as he opened the doors.

Mickey and his friends couldn't wait to go inside and get warm. The large, brightly lit building looked very inviting. And it was all decorated for Christmas with huge candy canes, beautiful green wreaths with red ribbons, and the cutest strings of colored lights! Donald had cozy visions of sipping a cup of piping hot chocolate in front of a crackling fire.

"Wow!" Mickey gasped when they stepped inside. "It's Santa's workshop!"

Sitting at workbenches all over the room, dozens of elves were building and painting toys as quickly as they could. Hundreds of toys—dolls, train sets, stuffed animals, and planes—lined shelves and spilled out of closets and toy chests.

Jitters handed them work smocks. Everyone thought it would be fun to help! Everyone, that is, except Donald.

Just then, the elves got very quiet. "Attention everyone," called Jitters, "Santa's coming."

Santa Claus appeared with a letter in hand. "I have *more* letters from children all over the world with their Christmas wishes," said Santa. "Last time I checked, every single doll, train, and whistle was spoken for. So, if we're going to make *all* the children happy this year, we'll have to work harder and pick up some speed! We've only got a few more hours before takeoff! Let's go, go, go! We can't disappoint the children!" cried Santa.

"We've worked so long without sleep, I don't know if we can make it," yawned a tired Jitters. "But I sure wouldn't want to leave anyone out...."

"What you need is more help," said Mickey. "And we're just the ones for the job!"

"I can sew," said Daisy.

"I guess I can make planes," offered Donald.

"And I can wrap, I think," yelled Goofy.

"That should do it," said Jitters. "With our new helpers and a little more elbow grease, we can finish up on time! So, everybody, get to work!"

"You can make trains," said Jitters as he took Mickey to a
workbench and showed him how to put a caboose together.

"Gosh, this will be a breeze!" laughed Mickey.

Before long, Mickey had ten trains ready to be painted
and inspected by the elves.

Minnie took care of the snow globes, shaking each one
to make sure it worked. Daisy was in charge of doll clothes.
She fastened snaps, tied sashes, and sewed on buttons!

Donald and Goofy, on the other hand, had some trouble
getting started.

But before long the elves had found just the right job for Goofy. He was having a swell time wrapping all the toys that Mickey, Minnie, and Daisy had made.

And Donald was busy driving the finished toys over to the elves for inspection, humming all the way!

Soon Santa returned to the workshop to check on everyone's progress. He added some color to a puppet's cheeks, and hammered a nail into a rocking horse. Now and then he glanced at the clock.

"It's five o'clock," Santa said. "Just one more hour to go." He was determined to be ready. "I know you can do it, and I'm counting on all of you to make this the best Christmas ever!"

"C'mon everyone," Mickey pleaded. "We've got to work faster!"

"Faster!" repeated Minnie, Daisy, Donald, and Goofy.

"Faster!" chanted the elves.

The workshop buzzed and clattered with sawing, hammering, painting, and wrapping.

Mickey looked at the clock. Five minutes. Four. Three. Two. One. As the clock chimed six, the last gifts sailed through the air and landed in Santa's sack.

But there was no time to celebrate. Now all those toys had to be loaded onto Santa's waiting sleigh. When every last toy was packed, Santa squeezed himself into the driver's seat and shook each helper's hand. When Mickey's turn came, Santa said, "You and your friends may not be elves, but you're the best helpers I've ever had. Thank you, all!"

"Say, how would you like to stay and be my honorary elves?" asked Santa.

"Gosh," said Mickey, "we might have to since Donald's plane is out of gas. We don't have a way home."

Santa thought for a moment. Then he snapped his fingers. "I know just what to do!" he said. "Jitters, lend these good folks my extra reindeer!" Then Santa took off with a wave and a jolly ho-ho-ho!

Moments later, Mickey and the gang climbed into their makeshift sleigh. "Look!" Minnie cried. "Presents from Santa for us!"

"Ready for takeoff!" Donald called to the reindeer—and up, up, up they went into the night sky.

Finally safe at home, everyone helped Mickey finish some last minute decorating.

"Can we open our presents from Santa now?" asked Daisy impatiently.

"You bet!" Mickey answered as they pulled off bows and tore open boxes. The friends looked at each other and burst out laughing. Each held up a brand-new elf suit in just the right size.

"Gawrsh," said Goofy. "It's what I've always wanted, and just my color, too!"